BEYOND BOMBAY HARBOUR, ACROSS THE BLUE WATERS, LIES THE GREEN ISLE OF ELEPHANTA. A SHORT WALK UPHILL TAKES YOU TO THE CAVE TEMPLES, CUT OUT OF SOLID ROCK BY THE HAND OF MAN. INSIDE THE MAIN CAVE MAY BE SEEN SOME OF THE FINEST SCULPTURES OF INDIAN ART CARVED ABOUT 1300 YEARS AGO.

WITH PIETY AND FAITH IN THEIR HEARTS AND SKILL IN THEIR FINGERS, PATIENTLY AND LABORIOUSLY, ARTISANS CREATED EXQUISITE WORKS OF ART FOR POSTERITY.

THESE CAVES WERE CARVED DURING THE REIGN OF THE MAURYAS OF THE KONKAN...

...WHO WERE DEFEATED IN A GREAT NAVAL BATTLE OFF ELEPHANTA BY THE CHALUKYAN KING, PULAKESIN II.

HAIL EMPEROR PULAKESIN!

AFTER BEING RULED BY SEVERAL HINDU DYNASTIES, THE ISLAND FELL TO THE SULTANS OF GUJARAT AND PASSED FROM THEM TO THE PORTUGUESE WHOSE SOLDIERS DAMAGED MANY OF THE SCULPTURES.

HA! HA! I HAVE HIT THE NOSE THIS TIME.

I HAVE DONE BETTER! I HAVE KNOCKED OFF AN ARM!

THE ISLAND WAS THEN TAKEN BY THE MARATHAS.

HAIL, EMPEROR SAMBHAJI!

WE SHALL MAKE THIS ISLAND AN INVINCIBLE FORT.

2

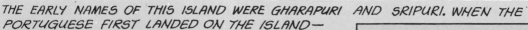

THE EARLY NAMES OF THIS ISLAND WERE GHARAPURI AND SRIPURI. WHEN THE PORTUGUESE FIRST LANDED ON THE ISLAND—

THIS IS UNIQUE! A STONE ELEPHANT TO RECEIVE US!

THE ISLAND SHOULD BE CALLED ELEPHANTA!

THE STONE ELEPHANT WAS LATER REMOVED BY THE BRITISH TO THE VICTORIA GARDENS+ AT BOMBAY.

BESIDES THE ELEPHANT, MANY OTHER ANTIQUITIES FROM THE ISLAND WERE REMOVED TO MUSEUMS—ONE OF THEM, A BEAUTIFUL FIGURE OF SADASHIVA, WAS TAKEN TO THE PRINCE OF WALES MUSEUM, BOMBAY.

OF THE SEVEN CAVES AT ELEPHANTA, THE MAIN CAVE IS THE MOST IMPORTANT. IT IS DEDICATED TO LORD SHIVA, THE GREAT GOD OF THE HINDU TRINITY.

+ NOW KNOWN AS VEERMATA JIJABAI BHONSLE UDYAN

IN THE MAIN CAVE, THE FIRST FIGURE AT THE RIGHT, IS THAT OF SHIVA AS NATARAJA.* HIS DANCE SYMBOLISES THE ETERNAL MOTION OF THE UNIVERSE.

LONG, LONG AGO, IN THE FOREST OF TARAGAM, THERE LIVED TEN THOUSAND RISHIS + WHO BY VIRTUE OF THEIR PENANCES HAD BECOME VERY POWERFUL.

WE ARE GREATER EVEN THAN THE DEVAS!

WE ARE INVINCIBLE!

AT KAILASA, SHIVA TURNED TO VISHNU.

YOU AND I MUST SUBDUE THESE ARROGANT SAGES.

SHIVA TOOK THE FORM OF A HANDSOME, YOUNG YOGI AND VISHNU THAT OF THE YOGI'S CHARMING WIFE.

THE RISHIS WILL FIND YOU IRRESISTIBLE!

AND YOU WILL CHARM THEIR WIVES!

* LORD OF DANCERS   + SAGES

AS SOON AS THEY APPEARED BEFORE THE RISHIS —

AH! WHO COULD THAT BEAUTY BE?

I CANNOT CONCENTRATE ON THE SACRIFICE.

SHE HAS DRIVEN THE MANTRAS OUT OF MY MIND.

LEAVING THE SACRIFICE UNFINISHED, THEY WALKED TOWARDS THE YOGI'S WIFE.

YOU WILL MARRY ME.

NO, SHE SHALL BE MINE.

NO, NO! MINE.

MEANWHILE, THE YOGI HAD THE SAME DISASTROUS EFFECT ON THEIR WIVES.

HE'S SURE TO CHOOSE ME!

HE WILL NOT! HE WILL CHOOSE ME.

AH, SIR, IF YOU WOULD BUT LOOK AT ME!

SUDDENLY THE RISHIS CAME TO THEIR SENSES.

WHAT HAS HAPPENED TO US?

AND OUR CHASTE WIVES!

THEY REALISED THAT THEY WERE BEING DELUDED BY SOME SUPERNATURAL POWER.

MAY YOU AND YOUR MAGICAL POWERS BE CURSED!

AND CURSED BE YOUR WIFE, THE SERPENT IN A WOMAN'S GUISE!

THEIR CURSES, HOWEVER, WERE OF NO AVAIL

SO THEY PREPARED A SACRIFICIAL FIRE.

WE WILL DESTROY THEM FOR ALL TIME.

THEY POURED GHEE INTO IT, CHANTING MANTRAS ALL THE WHILE.

SUDDENLY, A TIGER SPRANG FROM THE FIRE.

OUR CURSES MAY HAVE FAILED, BUT THIS TIGER WILL NOT. DESTROY HIM!

UNPERTURBED, SHIVA CAUGHT IT IN AN IRON GRIP...

...FLAYED IT...

...AND DRAPED ITS SKIN OVER HIS BODY.

THE NEXT MOMENT, A SNAKE EMERGED FROM THE FIRE...

...AND DARTED AT SHIVA.

HE CALMLY PICKED IT UP...

...AND WORE IT AS A GARLAND.

HARDLY HAD HE DONE SO WHEN, FROM THE FIRE, THERE EMERGED AN EVIL DWARF.

NOW TRY AND OVER-POWER HIM!

YOU CANNOT! HE IS THE EVIL GOBLIN HIM-SELF!

HE WILL DESTROY YOU!

IN REPLY, SHIVA DASHED THE EVIL CREATURE TO THE GROUND...

...ASSUMED HIS OWN FORM AND BEGAN TO DANCE. GOOD HAD TRIUMPHED OVER EVIL! THE RISHIS AND THE DEVAS IN HEAVEN GAZED IN AWE AND WONDER AT THE POWERFUL DANCE IN WHICH ALL CREATION AND THE COSMIC UNIVERSE WAS SET IN MOTION.

HE HAS TAUGHT US A LESSON IN HUMILITY!

GLORY TO THE GREAT SHIVA!

SHIVA'S WIFE, PARVATI, GAZED IN RAPTURE AT HER LORD. HIS BULL, NANDI, PLAYED THE DRUM. SAGE NARADA PLAYED THE TANPURA. BHRINGI, SHIVA'S DEVOTEE, DANCED WITH HIM IN GLEE.

WHO BUT MY LORD COULD DANCE LIKE THIS!

TANDU, SHIVA'S DISCIPLE, WAS AMAZED.

THE LORD HAS EXCELLED HIMSELF IN THIS DANCE. I MUST TEACH IT TO BHARATA *, MY TALENTED DISCIPLE.

THE HEARTS OF SHIVA'S SONS, GANESHA + AND KUMARA, BRIMMED WITH PRIDE.

NO ONE CAN DANCE LIKE HIM.

BRAHMA, THE CREATOR, CARRIED BY HIS FIVE SWANS, AND VISHNU ON GARUDA, HIS VEHICLE, LOOKED DOWN FROM THE HEAVENS IN JOY.

WHAT GRACE!

WHAT BEAUTY AND POWER!

* POPULARLY ACCEPTED AS THE AUTHOR OF NATYA SHASTRA, A VOLUMINOUS TREATISE ON DANCE AND DRAMA   + SEE AMAR CHITRA KATHA NO. 89

9

INDRA, SEATED ON HIS ELEPHANT, AIRAVATA, WATCHED IN WONDER. SHESHA, THE SERPENT, WAS ENCHANTED.

MAY I BE BORN AGAIN TO SEE THIS DANCE ONCE MORE!

AND ALL THOSE GATHERED THERE FELL AT SHIVA'S FEET AND BECAME HIS DEVOTEES.

PRAISE BE TO THE GREAT SHIVA!

THE NEXT PANEL IN THE MAIN CAVE DEPICTS THE KILLING OF THE DEMON ANDHAKA.

THE ASURA* ANDHAKA+ WAS THE SON OF SAGE KASHYAPA AND HIS WIFE DITI.

WHAT A STRONG SON I HAVE!

WOULD HE WERE GENTLE TOO!

WHEN ANDHAKA BECAME KING OF THE ASURAS, BY SEVERE PENANCES, HE PLEASED BRAHMA, THE CREATOR.

WHAT DO YOU WANT FROM ME?

MIGHT AND POWER, GREAT LORD! ALL SHOULD FEAR ME!

ANDHAKA THEN BEGAN HARASSING THE DEVAS. THEY FLED TO SHIVA FOR HELP.

BRAHMA GRANTED THE BOON AND VANISHED.

LORD, SAVE US FROM THAT ASURA!

HE WILL NOT LET US LIVE IN PEACE.

I WILL TEACH ANDHAKA A LESSON.

WHEN ANDHAKA LEARNT OF SHIVA'S INTENTIONS, HE SENT FOR THE EVIL NILA.

GO! DESTROY SHIVA!

BUT IN THE BATTLE BETWEEN SHIVA AND NILA, IT WAS THE LATTER WHO WAS SLAIN

*DEMON +SYMBOLISING DARKNESS AND IGNORANCE

MEANWHILE, ANDHAKA HAD SNEAKED INTO KAILASA TO CARRY AWAY PARVATI.

COME AWAY WITH ME. I AM GREATER THAN SHIVA.

GO AWAY FROM HERE, YOU EVIL DEMON!

AT THAT MOMENT, SHIVA RETURNED.

YOU HAVE GONE TOO FAR, ANDHAKA.

I AM READY TO RECEIVE YOUR ARROWS!

SHIVA'S ARROWS STRUCK THE ASURA, BUT EACH DROP OF BLOOD AS IT TOUCHED THE EARTH BECAME ANOTHER ASURA, FOR EVIL AND IGNORANCE ALWAYS MULTIPLY FAST. VISHNU CAME TO WATCH THIS COMBAT.

SHIVA NEEDS HELP.

ANDHAKA IS IMMORTAL!

ANDHAKA CAN NEVER DIE!

VISHNU RAISED HIS FINGER ...

... AND SENT HIS SUDARSHANA CHAKRA * FLYING.

YOU SHALL NEVER RISE AGAIN, EVIL ONES!

MEANWHILE, AS SHIVA ATTACKED AND KILLED ANDHAKA, HE MADE SURE THAT NOT A DROP OF BLOOD FELL TO THE GROUND, SO THAT NO NEW ASURAS WOULD SPRING UP.

* DISCUS

SHIVA, THE DESTROYER OF EVIL HAD VANQUISHED THE FORCES OF DARKNESS AND BROUGHT LIGHT INTO THE WORLD.

HAIL, LORD SHIVA !

IN ONE END OF THE MAIN CAVE IS THE SHRINE DEDICATED TO SHIVA IN THE FORM OF A LINGAM. IT IS GUARDED ON ALL SIDES BY DWARAPALAS*.

ONE DAY, BRAHMA, THE CREATOR, AND VISHNU, THE PRESERVER, WERE ARGUING ABOUT WHICH OF THEM WAS THE GREATER.

I AM THE CREATOR. THERE WOULD BE NO WORLD WITHOUT ME.

YOU MAY CREATE THE WORLD. BUT IT IS I WHO PRESERVE IT. I AM THE GREATER.

* GATE-KEEPERS

14

SUDDENLY, THERE APPEARED AN ENDLESS FIERY PILLAR, A LINGAM, WITHOUT BEGINNING OR END.

VISHNU, IN THE FORM OF A BOAR, BURROWED INTO THE EARTH.

I WILL FIND THE ORIGIN OF THIS LINGAM.

BRAHMA, IN THE FORM OF A SWAN, FLEW HIGHER AND HIGHER INTO THE HEAVENS.

AND I SHALL FIND THE END!

AFTER COUNTLESS YEARS, THE BOAR RETURNED EXHAUSTED.

I HAVE FAILED. I COULD NOT FIND ITS BEGINNING.

NEITHER DID BRAHMA SUCCEED IN HIS MISSION. BUT —

I MUST NOT ADMIT THAT I COULD NOT SEE THE END.

SUDDENLY HE SAW A KETAKI FLOWER FALL FROM THE HEAVENS.

YOU MUST COME WITH ME TO VISHNU AND SAY THAT I PICKED YOU UP FROM SHIVA'S HEAD.

TO PLEASE YOU, I WILL.

BRAHMA ASSUMED HIS REAL FORM AND WENT TO VISHNU ALONG WITH THE KETAKI FLOWER.

I SAW THE END OF THE FIERY LINGAM.

AND I WAS A WITNESS TO IT.

I BOW TO YOU, LORD BRAHMA. YOU ARE THE GREATEST OF US ALL.

SUDDENLY, SHIVA EMERGED FROM THE CENTRE OF THE FIERY LINGAM.

BRAHMA, YOU HAVE BEEN DISHONEST! FROM NOW ON, NONE SHALL HONOUR YOU. NOR WILL YOU HAVE YOUR OWN TEMPLE OR FESTIVAL.

AND YOU SHALL NO LONGER BE USED FOR WORSHIP IN MY TEMPLE.

YOU ARE WITHOUT BEGINNING AND HAVE NO END. IT IS OUT OF IGNORANCE THAT WE MADE THIS QUEST. FORGIVE US!

DEAR HARI, YOU ARE A LOVER OF TRUTH! I AM PLEASED WITH YOU. YOU WILL ALWAYS BE HONOURED AS I AM. YOU WILL HAVE SEPARATE TEMPLES AND FESTIVALS AND WILL BE LOVED BY THE PEOPLE AS I AM.

AND TO THIS DAY THERE ARE TEMPLES AND FESTIVALS CONNECTED WITH THE WORSHIP OF SHIVA AND VISHNU BUT FEW WORSHIP HIM WHO IS THE CREATOR.

ONE OF THE MOST EXQUISITE PANELS AT ELEPHANTA IS THAT OF THE MARRIAGE OF SHIVA AND PARVATI.

UMA* WAS THE DAUGHTER OF HIMAVAN+ AND MENA, HIS WIFE. THEY DOTED ON THEIR LOVELY DAUGHTER.

ONLY THE GREATEST OF KINGS IS GOOD ENOUGH FOR HER.

AND THE MOST HANDSOME!

BUT UMA HAD MADE HER OWN CHOICE.

I HAVE CHOSEN SHIVA.

* PARVATI   + THE HIMALAYAS

TO WOO AND WIN SHIVA, THE ASCETIC GOD, UMA TOOK TO MEDITATION...

...AND PRACTISED THE SEVEREST OF AUSTERITIES.

ONE DAY, AN OLD BRAHMANA APPEARED BEFORE HER.

YOU ARE YOUNG AND BEAUTIFUL. YOU SHOULD BE ENJOYING LIFE. AUSTERITIES ARE FOR THE OLD! WHY HAVE YOU RENOUNCED THE WORLD?

TO WIN THE LOVE OF SHIVA. I WISH TO MARRY HIM.

THAT MENDICANT?

HE HAS MATTED HAIR AND DECKS HIMSELF WITH SERPENTS! HE IS UNCOUTH AND...

HOW DARE YOU SPEAK OF MY LOVED ONE SO! GO AWAY!

SUDDENLY, THE OLD MAN CHANGED HIS FORM AND BEHOLD! IT WAS THE GREAT LORD HIMSELF.

IT IS YOU, MY LORD!

AND PARVATI WAS MARRIED TO SHIVA. HIMAVAN GAVE THE BRIDE AWAY. BRAHMA, THE CREATOR, ACTED AS PRIEST. VISHNU STOOD BY WATCHING THE BEAUTIFUL, SHY PARVATI WED THE GREAT SHIVA. MAINAKA, THE SON OF HIMAVAN, CARRIED THE CELESTIAL WATERS FOR THE CEREMONY.

THE NEXT PANEL IN THE MAIN CAVE IS OF SHIVA AS GANGADHARA * SHOWING THE DESCENT OF THE GANGA TO THE EARTH.

SAGARA, A GREAT RULER OF THE IKSHVAKU DYNASTY, HAD SIXTY THOUSAND WICKED SONS WHO CONSTANTLY HARASSED THE DEVAS AND THE RISHIS.

LET US DISTURB THAT RISHI IN MEDITATION.

LET US SHOOT AN ARROW BETWEEN THOSE TWO DEVAS.

ONCE SAGARA PERFORMED THE ASHWAMEDHA YAGNA ✝

LET THIS HORSE GO FORTH AND PROCLAIM THE GREATNESS OF SAGARA.

* THE ONE WHO HOLDS GANGA IN HIS MATTED LOCKS
✝ HORSE SACRIFICE

IN THE TRADITION OF THE TIMES, A KING WHO ASPIRED TO RULE THE WORLD WOULD LET LOOSE A HORSE WITH AUSPICIOUS MARKS. ANYONE WHO STOPPED THE HORSE WOULD BE CONSIDERED AN ENEMY AND WOULD BE ATTACKED BY THE ARMIES FOLLOWING THE HORSE. AFTER DEFEATING THE CHALLENGERS, IF ANY, THE HORSE WOULD BE BROUGHT BACK AND A YAGNA WOULD BE HELD TO CELEBRATE THE CONQUEST OF THE TERRITORIES TRAVERSED BY THE HORSE.

WE BOW TO SAGARA.

HE IS OUR EMPEROR.

INDRA, AFRAID THAT SAGARA WITH HIS GROWING POWER MIGHT DETHRONE HIM, STOLE THE HORSE AND LEFT IT IN THE HERMITAGE OF RISHI KAPILA.

SAGARA'S SONS WILL SOON TRACK DOWN THE HORSE AND...

AS WAS INTENDED, SAGARA'S SONS THOUGHT THAT KAPILA HAD STOLEN THE HORSE, AND RUSHED TO ATTACK HIM.

HOW DARE THIS OLD SAGE STEAL OUR FATHER'S HORSE!

HOW DARE THIS OLD FOOL SPOIL OUR FATHER'S HORSE SACRIFICE!

HE SHALL DIE FOR THIS!

THE NEXT MOMENT, THE POWERFUL SAGE OPENED HIS EYES IN ANGER AND REDUCED THEM TO ASHES.

MEANWHILE, WHEN HIS SONS DID NOT RETURN, SAGARA TURNED TO HIS GRANDSON, AMSHUMAN.

GO FORTH AND LOOK FOR YOUR UNCLES.

AMSHUMAN FOUND THE HORSE IN KAPILA'S ASHRAMA. THE SAGE WAS IMPRESSED BY THE YOUNG PRINCE.

ONLY THE PURIFYING TOUCH OF THE SACRED CELESTIAL RIVER GANGA CAN REDEEM THEM.

GANGA HAD TO BE BROUGHT DOWN TO THE EARTH. SAGARA AND AMSHUMAN FAILED IN THEIR EFFORTS. THEN AMSHUMAN'S SON, DILIPA TRIED. BUT —

MY PENANCES ARE NOT SEVERE ENOUGH. PERHAPS BHAGIRATHA WILL PROVE EQUAL TO THE TASK.

DILIPA'S SON, BHAGIRATHA, UNDER-TOOK SEVERE PENANCES TILL BRAHMA, THE CREATOR, STOOD BEFORE HIM.

I AM PLEASED. I SHALL SEND GANGA DOWN TO EARTH TO REDEEM YOUR ANCESTORS. BUT...

...SHIVA MUST BREAK HER FALL, OR THE EARTH WILL BE WASHED AWAY.

BHAGIRATHA UNDERTOOK FURTHER PENANCES TO PROPITIATE SHIVA.

PLEASE, MY LORD! BREAK THE FALL OF THE PROUD GANGA WHEN SHE COMES DOWN TO THE EARTH.

IT SHALL BE DONE.

AS SHE HURTLED DOWN FROM THE HEAVENS, SHIVA RECEIVED THE TURBULENT GANGA IN HIS MATTED LOCKS.

AMUSED BY GANGA'S ATTEMPTS TO ESCAPE, PARVATI STOOD BY, SMILING WITH PRIDE AT SHIVA'S STRENGTH.

THE FORCE OF GANGA'S FALL HAS BEEN BROKEN! SHE MAY NOW FLOW OVER THE ASHES OF MY ANCESTORS!

AS SOON AS GANGA FLOWED ONTO THE EARTH, THEN TO THE NETHER REGIONS AND OVER THE ASHES OF BHAGIRATHA'S ANCESTORS, THEY WERE BROUGHT BACK TO LIFE.

PRAISE BE TO OUR GREAT GRAND-CHILD, BHAGIRATHA!

PRAISE BE TO SHIVA FOR RELEASING US!

BRAHMA AND SHIVA THEN BLESSED BHAGIRATHA.

YOU WILL ALWAYS BE REMEMBERED FOR YOUR STRENGTH OF PURPOSE.

YOUR EFFORTS WILL BE A HOUSE-HOLD WORD FOR ALL TIME.

EVEN TO THIS DAY A DIFFICULT TASK WHICH IS ACHIEVED BY SUPERHUMAN EFFORT IS CALLED A BHAGIRATHA PRAYATNA*.

* EFFORT OF BHAGIRATHA

IN THE CENTRE OF THE NORTHERN WALL IS THE GIGANTIC FIGURE OF SHIVA AS MAHESHA, THE SUPREME GOD, COMBINING IN HIMSELF THE QUALITIES OF CREATOR, PRESERVER AND DESTROYER. IN THE CENTRE IS SHIVA, THE CREATOR, HOLDING A MATULUNGA,* THE SYMBOL OF CREATION. ON OUR RIGHT IS SHIVA, THE PRESERVER, HOLDING A LOTUS. ON OUR LEFT IS SHIVA AS RUDRA, THE DESTROYER, HOLDING A COBRA. YET OUT OF DESTRUCTION COMES CREATION AND THE CYCLE OF LIFE.

* A CITRUS FRUIT

THE NEXT PANEL IS THAT OF ARDHANARISHWARA SHIVA, WHEN SHIVA BECAME ONE WITH HIS WIFE, PARVATI, SYMBOLISING THE UNITY OF THE MALE AND THE FEMALE ELEMENTS IN THE UNIVERSE.

THE PANEL BEYOND SHOWS A DOMESTIC SCENE WITH SHIVA AND PARVATI ON MOUNT KAILASA. PARVATI, PRETENDING TO BE ANGRY, TURNS HER FACE AWAY FROM SHIVA.

THE NEXT PANEL SHOWS THE DEMON-KING, RAVANA, OVERCOME WITH PRIDE IN HIS OWN POWER, ATTEMPTING TO UPROOT AND LIFT MOUNT KAILASA.

I HAVE DONE IT! I AM STRONGER THAN SHIVA HIMSELF!

AS THE MOUNTAIN SHOOK, PARVATI TREMBLED WITH FEAR, BUT SHIVA SMILED.

RAVANA WILL DESTROY US.

AN ARROGANT MAN IS HIS OWN ENEMY. FEAR NOT!

AND PRESSING THE MOUNTAIN DOWN WITH HIS FOOT, SHIVA IMPRISONED RAVANA.

THIS SCULPTURE ALSO SHOWS SHIVA WITH HIS THREE EYES, THE THIRD EYE BEING THE EYE OF ANGER.

ONCE, WHEN SHIVA AND PARVATI WERE ON MOUNT KAILASA, PARVATI PLAYFULLY WENT BEHIND HIM AND CLOSED BOTH HIS EYES.

SHE THEREBY SHUT OUT THE LIGHT IN THE THREE WORLDS AND ALL LIVING THINGS BEGAN TO PERISH.

THE SUN HAS DISAPPEARED!

THE EARTH IS PLUNGED IN DARKNESS!

BUT A THIRD EYE APPEARED ON SHIVA'S FOREHEAD, ABOVE PARVATI'S HANDS...

...AND THE UNIVERSE WAS SAVED.

THE GREAT SHIVA HAS SAVED US!

OM NAMAH SHIVAYA!

THE LAST PANEL IN THE MAIN CAVE SHOWS SHIVA AS THE GREAT YOGI. HE SITS ON A LOTUS IN MEDITATION. BRAHMA, THE CREATOR, AND INDRA, THE KING OF THE DEVAS GAZE UPON HIM. LIKE THE LOTUS, PURE AND CLEAN, THOUGH IT GROWS IN MUDDY WATERS, HIS FACE REFLECTS THE CALM AND SPIRITUAL STRENGTH OF THE YOGI.

BEYOND, FACING THE LINGAM SHRINE, IS A PEDESTAL WHERE ONCE STOOD NANDI, SHIVA'S VEHICLE, THE BULL.

THERE ARE SIX OTHER CAVES ON ELEPHANTA. ALL OF THEM BEAR TESTIMONY TO THE SKILL AND TALENT OF OUR ANCIENT ARCHITECTS AND SCULPTORS. RENOWNED, YET HUMBLE IN THEIR WORSHIP OF THE LORD, THESE CRAFTSMEN TRANSLATED INTO REALITY THE GRANDEUR, THE POWER AND THE BEAUTY OF THE GREAT SHIVA, THE AUSPICIOUS ONE, THE LORD OF THE THREE WORLDS.

SUBSCRIBE NOW!

Pay only ₹~~1080~~ 800!

25% OFF

A twelve month subscription to TINKLE and TINKLE DIGEST

YOUR DETAILS*

Student's Name _____

Parent's Name _____

Date of Birth: _____ (DD MM YYYY)

Address: _____

_____

City: _____ PIN: _____

State: _____

School: _____

Class: _____

Email (Student): _____

Email (Parent): _____

Tel of Parent: (R): _____

Mobile: _____

Parent's Signature:

*All the above fields are mandatory for the subscription to get activated.

PAYMENT OPTIONS

☐ **Credit Card**
Card Type: Visa ☐ MasterCard ☐
Please charge ₹800 to my Credit Card Number
below: ☐☐☐☐ ☐☐☐☐ ☐☐☐☐ ☐☐☐☐
Expiry Date: ☐☐ ☐☐

Cardmember's Signature:

☐ **CHEQUE / DD**
Enclosed please find cheque / DD no. ☐☐☐☐☐☐ drawn i
favour of "ACK Media Direct Pvt. Ltd."
on (bank) _____,
for the amount _____, dated ☐☐/☐☐/☐☐☐☐ and
send it to: **IBH magazine Service, Arch no.30, Below
Mahalaxmi Bridge, Near Racecourse, Mahalaxmi,
Mumbai 400034**

☐ **Pay by VPP**
Please pay the ₹800 to the postman on the delivery
of 1st issue. (Additional charges ₹30 apply)

☐ **Online subscription**
Visit www.amarchitrakatha.com

For any queries or further information please
write to us ACK Media Direct Pvt. Ltd.,
Krishna House, 3rd Floor, Raghuvanshi Mills Compund,
Senapati Bapat Marg, Lower Parel, Mumbai 400 013.
Tel: 022-40 49 74 36
or send us an Email at customercare@ack-media.com

WHICH OF THE ACKS HAVE YOU STILL NOT READ?

ACK EPICS AND MYTHOLOGY

Best known stories from the Epics and the Puranas

ABHIMANYU
ANDHAKA
ANIRUDDHA
ARJUNA, TALES OF
ARUNI AND UTTANKA
ASHWINI KUMARS
AYYAPPAN
BAHUBALI
BALARAMA, TALES OF
BHEEMA AND HANUMAN
BHEESHMA
CHANDRAHASA
CHURNING OF THE OCEAN
DASHARATHA
DHRUVA AND ASHTAVAKRA
DRAUPADI
DRONA
DURGA, TALES OF
ELEPHANTA
GANDHARI
GANESHA
GANGA
GARUDA
GHATOTKACHA
GITA, THE
GOLDEN MONGOOSE, THE
HANUMAN
HANUMAN TO THE RESCUE
HARISCHANDRA
INDRA AND SHACHI
INDRA AND SHIBI
JAGANNATHA OF PURI
JAYADRATHA
KACHA AND DEVAYANI
KARNA
KARTTIKEYA
KRISHNA
KRISHNA AND JARASANDHA
KRISHNA AND NARAKASURA
KRISHNA AND RUKMINI
KRISHNA AND SHISHUPALA
KRISHNA AND THE FALSE
VAASUDEVA
KUMBHAKARNA
LORD OF LANKA, THE
MAHABHARATA
MAHIRAVANA
NACHIKETA
NAHUSHA
NALA DAMAYANTI
NARADA, TALES OF
PANDAVA PRINCES, THE
PANDAVAS IN THE HIDING, THE
PRAHLAD
RAMA
RAVANA HUMBLED
SATI AND SHIVA
SAVITRI
SHIVA PARVATI
SHIVA, TALES OF
SONS OF RAMA, THE
SUDAMA
SURYA
SYAMANTAKA GEM, THE
TRIPURA
ULOOPI
UPANISHADS, TALES FROM
VALI
VISHNU, TALES OF
VISHWAMITRA

YAYATI
YUDHISHTHIRA, TALES OF

ACK INDIAN CLASSICS

Enchanting tales from Indian literature

ANANDA MATH
ANCESTORS OF RAMA
DEVI CHOUDHURANI
KANNAGI
KAPALA KUNDALA
MALAVIKA
RATNAVALI
SHAKUNTALA
UDAYANA
URVASHI
VASANTASENA
VASAVADATTA

ACK FABLES AND HUMOUR

Evergreen folktales, legends and tales of wisdom and humour

ACROBAT AND OTHER
   BUDDHIST TALES, THE
ADVENTURES OF
   AGAD DATTA, THE
ADVENTURES OF
   BADDU AND CHHOTU, THE
AMRAPALI
ANGULIMALA
BAG OF GOLD COINS, A
BATTLE OF WITS
BIKAL THE TERRIBLE
BIRBAL STORIES
   BIRBAL THE CLEVER
   BIRBAL THE GENIUS
   BIRBAL THE JUST
   BIRBAL THE WISE
   BIRBAL THE WITTY
   BIRBAL TO THE RESCUE
   THE INIMITABLE BIRBAL
CELESTIAL NECKLACE, THE
CHANDRALALAT
COWHERD OF ALAWI, THE
FEARLESS BOY AND OTHER
   BUDDHIST TALES, THE
FOOL'S DISCIPLES, THE
FRIENDS AND FOES
GOPAL AND THE COWHERD
GOPAL THE JESTER
HITOPADESHA TALES
   CHOICE OF FRIENDS
   HOW FRIENDS ARE PARTED
JATAKA TALES
   BIRD STORIES
   DEADLY FEAST, THE
   DEER STORIES
   ELEPHANT STORIES
   GIANT & THE DWARF, THE
   HIDDEN TREASURE, THE
   JACKAL STORIES
   MAGIC CHANT, THE
   MONKEY STORIES
   MOUSE MERCHANT, THE
   NANDIVISHALA
   STORIES OF COURAGE
   STORIES OF WISDOM
   TALES OF MISERS
   TRUE FRIENDS
KESARI THE FLYING THIEF
KING KUSHA
LEARNED PANDIT, THE

MAGIC GROVE, THE
MARYADA RAMA, TALES OF
PANCHATANTRA TALES
   BRAHMIN & THE GOAT
   CROWS AND OWLS
   DULLARD AND OTHER
      STORIES
   GREEDY MOTHER-IN-LAW, THE
   HOW THE JACKAL ATE THE
      ELEPHANT
   JACKAL & THE
      WAR DRUM, THE
   PRICELESS GEM, THE
   PRINCE AND THE
      MAGICIAN
   QUEEN'S NECKLACE, THE
   PANDIT AND THE MILKMAID
RAMAN OF TENALI
RAMAN THE MATCHLESS WIT
SAKSHI GOPAL
SHRENIK
TIGER & THE WOODPECKER,
TIGER-EATER, THE
VIKRAMADITYA'S THRONE

ACK BRAVEHEARTS

Stirring tales of brave men and women of India

AJATASHATRU
AKBAR
AMAR SINGH RATHOR
ASHOKA
BAGHA JATIN
BAJI RAO I
BALADITYA & YASHODHARMA
BANDA BAHADUR
BAPPA RAWAL
BENI MADHO AND PIR ALI
BHAGAT SINGH
BIMBISARA
CHAND BIBI
CHANDRA SHEKHAR AZAD
CHANDRAGUPTA MAURYA
DURGADAS
ELLORA CAVES
HARSHA
HISTORIC CITY OF DELHI, THE
JAHANGIR
JALLIANWALA BAGH
KALPANA CHAWLA
KRISHNADEVA RAYA
KUNWAR SINGH
LACHIT BARPHUKAN
LALITADITYA
MANGAL PANDE
NOOR JAHAN
PADMINI
PANNA AND HADI RANI
PAURAVA AND ALEXANDER
PRITHVIRAJ CHAUHAN
RAJA BHOJA
RAJA RAJA CHOLA
RANA KUMBHA
RANA PRATAP
RANA SANGA
RANI ABBAKKA
RANI DURGAVATI
RANI OF JHANSI
RANJIT SINGH
RASH BEHARI BOSE
SAMUDRA GUPTA
SEA ROUTE TO INDIA
SHAH JAHAN
SHALIVAHANA

SHER SHAH
SHIVAJI
SHIVAJI, TALES OF
SUBHAS CHANDRA BOSE
SULTANA RAZIA
TANAJI
THE RANI OF KITTUR
TIPU SULTAN
VEER HAMMIR
VEER SAVARKAR
VELU THAMPI
VIKRAMADITYA

ACK VISIONARIES

Inspiring tales of thinkers, social reformers and nation builders

ADI SHANKARA
AMBEDKAR, BABASAHEB
BASAVESHWARA
BIRLA G.D.
BUDDHA
CHANAKYA
CHAITANYA MAHAPRABHU
CHINMAYANANDA, SWAMI
CHOKHA MELA
DAYANANDA
DESHBANDHU
   CHITTANRANJAN DAS
FA HIEN
GURU ARJAN
GURU GOBIND SINGH
GURU NANAK
GURU TEGH BAHADUR
HIUEN TSANG
J.R.D.TATA
JAGADIS CHANDRA BOSE
JAMSETJI TATA
JAWAHARLAL NEHRU
JAYAPRAKASH NARAYAN
JNANESHWAR
KABIR
KALIDASA
LAL BAHADUR SHASTRI
LOKAMANYA TILAK
MADHVACHARYA
MAHAVIRA
MEGASTHENES
MIRABAI
MOTHER TERESA
PRANAVANANDA, SWAMI
RABINDRANATH TAGORE
RAMAKRISHNA, SRI
RAMANA MAHARSHI
RAMANUJA
RAM SHASTRI
SAIBABA, TALES OF
SHANKAR DEV
SOORDAS
SUBRAMANIA BHARATI
TANSEN
TULSIDAS
VIDYASAGAR
VIVEKANANDA
ZARATHUSHTRA

ACK SPECIAL ISSUES

BHAGAWAT - THE KRISHNA AVATAR
DASHA AVATAR
JESUS CHRIST
MAHABHARATA
MAHATMA GANDHI
RAM CHARIT MANAS
VALMIKI'S RAMAYANA

 All titles available on www.AmarChitraKatha.com

ELEPHANTA

Lord Shiva, it is believed, has many faces and multiple forms, and
each tells a tale. Visitors to an emerald-green island off the coast of
Mumbai are reminded of these dramatic episodes by the work of
skilful, dedicated sculptors, who lived more than 1,300 years ago!
Their carvings have survived in the caves of Elephanta, despite the
ravages of time and vandals and destroying armies.

OTHER ACK EPICS & MYTHOLOGY:

  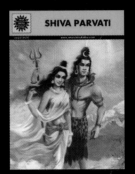 

GANGA TALES OF SHIVA SHIVA PARVATI TRIPURA

ALSO LOOK FOR:

   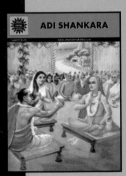

AJATASHATRU URVASHI A BAG OF GOLD COINS ADI SHANKARA

BRAVEHEARTS INDIAN CLASSICS FABLES & HUMOUR VISIONARIES

www.ack-media.com

ISBN 81-89999-40-0

What kind of church should we be?

GOSPEL SHAPED

MERCY

Stephen Um

A gospel shaped church.